For the Bourdon-Hadley family –
Don and Margie, Sarah and Caley –
who showed me the mountains where the ghost train runs – P Y

To Carly, Karen and Eric – H C

Text copyright © 1996 by Paul Yee
Illustrations copyright © 1996 by Harvey Chan
11 10 09 08 07   5 6 7 8 9

Groundwood Books / House of Anansi Press
110 Spadina Avenue, Suite 801, Toronto, Ontario M5V 2K4
Distributed in the USA by Publishers Group West
1700 Fourth Street, Berkeley, CA 94710

We acknowledge for their financial support of our publishing program the Canada Council for the Arts,
the Government of Canada through the Book Publishing Industry Development Program (BPIDP)
and the Ontario Arts Council.

ONTARIO ARTS COUNCIL
CONSEIL DES ARTS DE L'ONTARIO

Library and Archives Canada Cataloguing in Publication

Yee, Paul
Ghost Train
ISBN-13: 978-0-88899-257-4
ISBN-10: 0-88899-257-2
1. Picture books for children. I. Chan, Harvey.
II. Title
PS8597.E3G56 1996   jC813'.54   C96-930018-2

The illustrations are done in oils. The front and end pieces are drypoint etchings on copper.
Book design by Michael Solomon
Printed in China by Everbest Printing Co. Ltd.

Ghost Train

PAUL YEE

PICTURES BY

HARVEY CHAN

GROUNDWOOD BOOKS

HOUSE OF ANANSI PRESS

TORONTO / BERKELEY

ONE day long ago, a girl named Choon-yi was born to poor peasants in South China. Alas, she arrived with only one arm, which greatly horrified her mother. But Choon-yi's father loved his daughter dearly. He made sure that her childhood days were happy ones, even though the family owned no land and had only a few scrawny pigs to tend.

The villagers soon discovered that Choon-yi's one arm was no ordinary limb. When she held an ink brush, the pictures she painted looked as real as life. The flowers she colored seemed to give off fragrance. The animals she sketched seemed to breathe and move. On market days in town, she sat outside with ink and paper, offering to draw people's faces for a fee.

Still there was not enough money to rent land and pay taxes. Choon-yi's family often went to bed hungry. When she was twelve years old, her father decided to sail to North America, where companies were hiring workers to build a railway through the mountains.

Choon-yi and her mother were worried, for the work was well known to be dangerous. When it came time to leave, Choon-yi's father held her close and whispered, "Don't cry, Daughter. I promise you we will soon be reunited. And together we will paint a picture."

Choon-yi nodded sadly and bade her father farewell. For two years he sent money and messages home. He told how he missed them and described how the mountains around him touched the clouds. Rivers shot like fiery silver dragons through steep canyons, but dynamite accidents were common. He and his friends gathered around the campfire at nights to keep the loneliness away.

Then one day a letter came enclosing a large sum of money.

"Choon-yi, my daughter, come quick!" her father's words said. "Bring your ink brushes and your colors. Bring a roll of the finest paper you can find!"

Choon-yi tied her belongings into a carrying sash and sailed on the next ship to North America. In the bustling port city, she hurried to the company office to ask where her father worked.

The paymaster checked his ledger and looked up grimly.

"I am sorry, child, but your father was killed last week," he said. "The side of the mountain collapsed and carried his crew into the river far below. No bodies were found."

He handed her a final pay packet and turned away.

Choon-yi wept bitterly and trudged back to the ship. But the night before it sailed to China, her father came to her in a dream.

"Paint me the fire-car, Daughter!" he pleaded, waving blood-stained hands. "Paint me the train that runs on the road I built."

Choon-yi awoke with a start and left the ship immediately. Her first task was to find a fire-car, for never before had she seen a train. She did not know if it was big or small, tall or short, round or square.

So she set out for the train station. But without a ticket, she could not reach the boarding platform. She approached the stationmaster for help, but she knew no English. She stepped outside, but high wooden fences blocked her view.

A loud snorting and a ferocious chugging could be heard. Choon-yi peered through a knothole and caught a glimpse of a great iron barrel, puffs of smoke, huge, heavy wheels and a long row of windows.

Off she went to paint what she had seen. But when she had finished, she shook her head. This was not the fire-car her father had asked for.

So she set out and climbed a hill overlooking the railway tracks. In the distance she heard a steam whistle and a steady *clickety-clack* growing louder and louder. Then the fire-car swung into view under a plume of smoke, pulling a long chain of wheeled boxes like a huge snake slithering across a field.

Off Choon-yi went to paint what she had seen. But when she had finished, she shook her head. The angles were distorted and the details fuzzy. This was not the fire-car her father had wanted.

So she set out and bought a ticket to ride the train herself. She stepped aboard, eyes eager with anticipation, and saw everything: the painted numbers on each car, the polished wooden steps, the dark oil clinging to the wheel axles.

At every stop Choon-yi went out and walked around the fire-car. She peered at the undercarriage, she poked at the giant hooks linking the cars, and she stared at the engineer, who stared right back.

All afternoon she rode the train, swaying to its gentle roll. She let her mind's eye recall every detail: the inverted cone atop the chimney, the bars of the fanlike grill, the bolts binding the beast together.

It was dark when Choon-yi changed trains for the trip back. Into the deep night the engine hurtled. On both sides trees and mountains were silhouetted high against a moonlit sky.

Choon-yi dozed fitfully, but suddenly she heard a moaning shriek, then groans of agony!

She jumped up. She looked out the window but saw nothing. No one else sat in the car. She clapped her hand over her ear, but the anguished wailing did not cease.

Sometimes the moaning was one voice. At other times it was a chorus of many. She could make no sense of the words, but pain oozed from the cries like blood flowing from a wound.

Choon-yi hugged herself tight and repeated, "I am not afraid. I have hurt no one."

When the train finally pulled into town, she fled from the station, vowing never to ride the train again. She planned to finish the painting and leave for home immediately.

Off she went to paint what she had seen. This time the train that emerged from the brushstrokes held true to all she had seen and felt. The engine's gleaming chimneys unfurled a swirl of smoke over powerful crankshafts that drove the great wheels. The windows on the passenger cars sparkled clear, and the painted trim was fresh and sharp. The railway cut a sleek ribbon through the mountains, with jagged canyons yawning below.

That night, Choon-yi slept deeply. Then her father came in a dream, walking toward her over the railway ties.

"Daughter, you've made a masterpiece!" he called out, smiling and opening his arms as if to hug her. "Listen to me and do as I say. Tomorrow, follow the railway tracks far out of the city. At dusk, as the sun slips below the horizon, lay your painting open between the steel tracks. Light three big sticks of incense and plant them firmly. Then stand back!"

The next day, Choon-yi rolled up her painting and tied it to her back. She followed the steel trail out of town, passing farms to enter the forests. At dusk, she knelt and spread her work open between the tracks. She lit three thick sticks of incense, and then ran far back.

The red-gold rays of the setting sun cut through the incense, hitting the colors on the paper and setting them aglow. The inks and pigments began to swirl and dance amidst the dense smoke. But the darkness of night made it hard to see, and when Choon-yi ran up for a closer look, lo and behold! The train from her painting had swelled up like a balloon and come alive.

Choon-yi slowly extended her hand and touched a hot, pulsating engine and solid metal. She gasped and fell back. What magic was this?

Then she felt someone behind her. She turned, and there stood her father.

"Ba!" she cried.

"Daughter, you've done well," he said, smiling to show his bright white teeth. But when Choon-yi ran toward him, he shook his head and stopped her. "You mustn't touch me. I have left your world."

Tears streamed from Choon-yi, but Ba called out cheerfully. "Come, Daughter! Let's ride this train!"

Choon-yi held back. "But why, Ba?" she asked fearfully.

Her father was already striding toward the throbbing machine. "You heard the moaning when you rode the train, did you not?"

Choon-yi nodded and stumbled after him.

"Many men died building this railway," Ba said. "All along the route, bodies have been swept away by the river or buried under a landslide. Their bones will never be recovered. But the time has come to transport their souls home."

Choon-yi walked through the empty cars and joined Ba in the engine. As the train sped into the night, she peered out into the darkness, lit only by the moon above. A mist hung over the cold earth, and Choon-yi saw shadows and figures gliding through the haze. The train streaked into long dark tunnels and crossed bridges over icy rivers. This time, she heard no moaning.

"Go through the cars," Ba told her. "But don't touch anyone."

Walking through the train now, Choon-yi found it filled with men. Their clothing was torn and dirty, stained with mud and blood. Some sat in circles playing dominoes and talking. Some passed around a water-pipe. Others stood at the windows, watching the landscape with longing eyes. Still others walked impatiently up and down the length of the car, hands held behind their backs, muttering anxiously to themselves.

As more and more men came aboard, they hailed each other with hearty welcomes.

Choon-yi's eyes welled with tears. The men talked of their families, about how they longed to see them. They talked of hopes and dreams, about what they had planned to do with their earnings. They talked of work, about how each day had been a question of life or death.

Soon Choon-yi fell asleep. Her feet were tired from walking. Her eyes were tired from crying. Her father came to her again.

"Daughter, you have done well," Ba said. "Now roll up the painting and take it home to China. Then climb the highest hill in the region and burn it. Let our ashes sail on the four winds. That way our souls will finally find their way home."

Choon-yi awoke with a start. It was dawn, and she was lying on the ground by the tracks. She rubbed her eyes. Had she really gone for a ride on the ghost train? Or had it all been a dream?

She picked up her painting. The train stood just as she had drawn it. But when she looked closer, now she saw faces framed in every window! And there stood Ba, waving from the spot where the engineer usually stood!